This Book

Belongs to:

sam

....

BARYONYX

CERATOSAURUS

IGUANODON

VELOCIRAPTOR

PACHYCEPHALOSAURUS

STYRACOSAURUS

DILOPHOSAURUS

CARNOTAURUS

TRICERATOPS

STEGOSAURUS

Dear Customer!

Thank you for your recent purchase, we hope you love it!

If you do, would you consider posting an online review?

This helps us to continue providing great products and helps potential buyers to make confident decisions.

Thank you in advance for your review and for being a preferred customer.

See more of my books!   Michael Blackmore

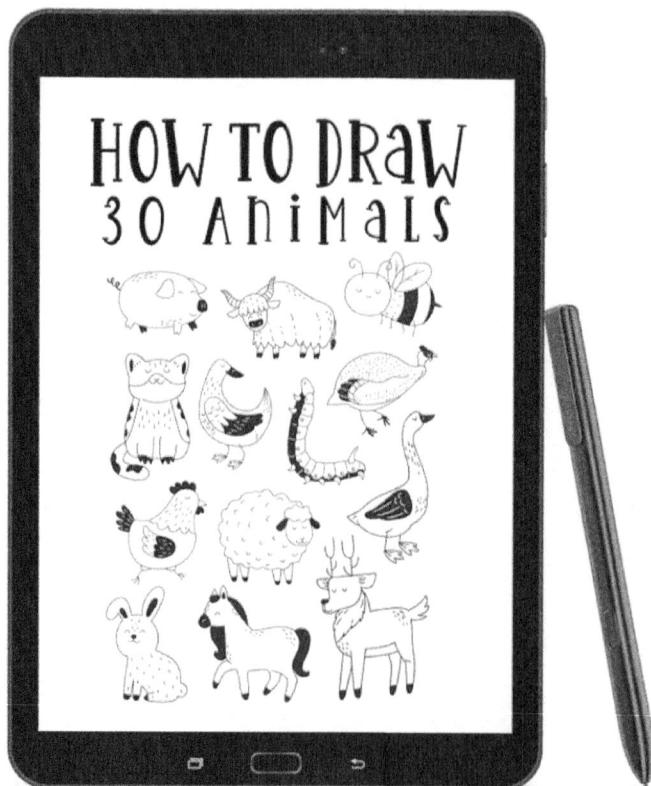

FREE GiFT FOR YOU!

scan Me!

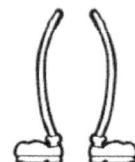

Printed in Great Britain
by Amazon